The Wrong Pong

By Rebecca Lisle

Illustrated by Amy Lane

Bertie loved being at Wizard School. He wanted to become a great wizard, so he always tried very hard.

One day, Big Wizard gave Bertie's class a new challenge.

"As you may know, Prince Casper has been asleep for a whole month," Big Wizard said.

"No one can wake him, so the queen has asked us to make a magic Wake-Up Potion."

Bertie was excited. He loved making magic potions.

"And," Big Wizard continued, "the king and queen will award a gold wand to the wizard who wakes Prince Casper!"

"Oooh!" cried the wizards. They all wanted the gold wand. They hurried off to the potion room to start making their magic potions.

The wizards got to work. Bertie chose a green bottle from the cupboard. Now, to begin!

Around him, all the other wizards were hard at work. Another wizard called Sid was sitting next to Bertie. Sid really wanted that gold wand. He watched Bertie closely.

"What are you putting in your potion?" Sid asked.

"Rose petals, so it smells nice," Bertie said. "And 'wake-up' crystals, obviously!"

"Obviously!" Sid agreed, adding them to his own cauldron.

Bertie put in a drop of 'eye-opener' potion and three drops of 'alarm-clock' essence. He mixed in a sprinkling of 'bird song' and just a touch of 'lightning and thunder', but not too much – he didn't want to scare Prince Casper!

Bertie said some magic words as he mixed his ingredients together.

He strained the potion and put it in the green bottle.

Then he put it on the windowsill to gather sunlight and went off to his next lesson. He knew his potion would be great.

Sid stared at Bertie's bottle of Wake-Up Potion. "I bet it's better than mine," he said to himself. When no one was looking, he opened Bertie's bottle and added five drops of 'stinky smell' potion, four drops of 'super stench', and a pinch of 'powerful pong' powder. Sid had to put a peg on his nose because the smell was SO dreadful!

"Let's add more pongs," he said with a grin.

"How about some 'terrible tang' and a

teaspoon of 'vomit vapour'... Yuck!

This potion smells disgusting!"

'Bertie won't win that gold wand, I will!'

Sid thought. 'But what if one of the other

wizards has made a potion better than mine?

I must win that gold wand!'

When the potion room was empty, Sid sneaked back in. First, he tossed the spell books and pencils around. Then he knocked over all the stools and tipped over every bottle of Wake-Up Potion – except for his and Bertie's. Bertie's magic potion couldn't possibly win – it was too stinky!

Then, Sid ran out of the potion room shouting, "Help! It's a disaster! A dragon has got into the workshop! All the potions have been spilled!"

In the end, only Bertie and Sid had magic potions to take to the castle.

"Welcome, welcome!" the queen said, ushering them in. "Only two wizards?"

"There was an accident," Sid told her.

"Oh! What bad luck!" she cried.

"Well, let's hope one of you has a potion that will wake Prince Casper," said the king.

"You first, Bertie," Sid said.

Sid couldn't help smirking. 'This should be fun,' he thought, 'and I'll win the gold wand!'

Bertie handed his bottle of potion to the king. The king took the stopper out. There was the crash of distant thunder, birds singing, alarm bells ringing and a terrible, terrible PONG!

"Yuck!" the king cried. "That is disgusting!"

He held his nose and put the stopper back in.

"What were you thinking, Bertie?"

Bertie was horrified. "But I..."

"It can't be that bad," the queen said. She took the bottle and smelt it too. "Ugh!" she yelled. She jammed the stopper back. "Take this pong away, Bertie!"

"Well, really!" snapped the king. "How could you bring such a dreadful stink to our castle?!"

"I'm sorry," Bertie said, putting his bottle of Wake-Up Potion in his cloak pocket. "I don't understand what went wrong."

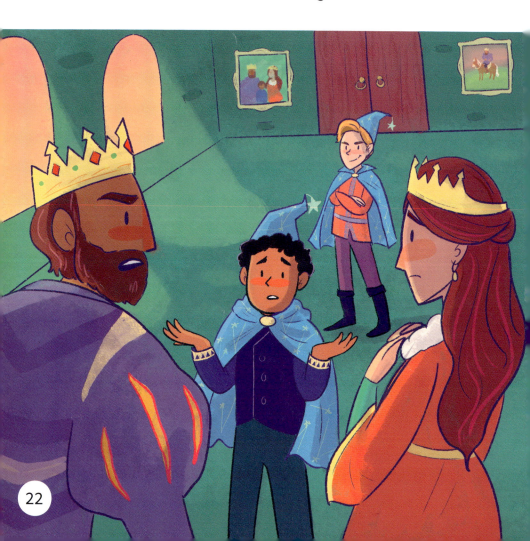

Then he looked at Sid and saw how he was grinning! Bertie guessed Sid had done this. Sneaky Sid!

The queen sniffed Sid's potion. "Your potion smells lovely," she said. "Let's try it."

They trooped upstairs to the prince's chamber.

Prince Casper lay fast asleep on his huge bed, snoring.

"A terrible spell has done this to him," the king said, shaking his head.

"Your potion must work!" said the queen.

"It *will* work," Sid said, confidently. He'd put in all the same things as Bertie – without the stinks!

Sid opened his potion bottle. The scent of roses filled the air. Birds twittered, an alarm bell jingled, but...

Nothing. The prince's eyelids did not even flutter. The queen burst into tears. "My poor boy! He'll never wake again!" she cried.

Suddenly, Bertie had an idea. He tiptoed up to the bedside, opened his potion bottle and wafted the stinky potion under the prince's nose.

"Yuck!" Prince Casper cried, leaping out of bed.

"What an awful pong!" he yelled, holding his nose.

"Oh, hello Mum. Hello Dad! What's for breakfast? I'm famished."

"He's awake!" cheered the queen. "Thank you, Bertie!"

"Hooray!" cried Bertie.

"But, but it's not fair!" Sid sulked.

"What's not fair?" the king asked.

"Oh, er, nothing," mumbled Sid.

They all went downstairs, where plates and dishes piled with food were brought in for Prince Casper. He ate it all.

The king and queen thanked Bertie again and apologised for being rude about his smelly potion.

"Here is the gold wand we promised," the king said, handing Bertie a beautiful golden wand. "Thank you, and congratulations!"

Sid sneered.

"Well done!" shouted the prince. "Thank you for waking me from the spell, Bertie. Though that pong was awful!"

"Well," Bertie said with a grin, "I guess the wrong pong was the right pong in the end!"

Quiz

1. How long was Prince Casper asleep for?
a) A month
b) A year
c) A week

2. What was the prize for waking Prince Casper?
a) A silver trophy
b) A gold wand
c) A gold hat

3. What did Sid do to Bertie's potion?
a) He made it smelly
b) He spilt it
c) He made it purple

4. What did Sid's potion smell like?
a) Grass
b) Sweets
c) Roses

5. What woke Prince Casper up?
a) Sid's potion
b) The smell of food
c) Bertie's smelly potion

Turn over for answers

Book Bands for Guided Reading

The Institute of Education book banding system is a scale of colours that reflects the various levels of reading difficulty. The bands are assigned by taking into account the content, the language style, the layout and phonics. Word, phrase and sentence level work is also taken into consideration.

Maverick Early Readers are a bright, attractive range of books covering the pink to white bands. All of these books have been book banded for guided reading to the industry standard and edited by a leading educational consultant.

To view the whole Maverick Readers scheme, visit our website at
www.maverickearlyreaders.com

Or scan the QR code above to view our scheme instantly!

Quiz Answers: 1a, 2b, 3a, 4c, 5c